*Murder by UFO*

Charlie Sands was investigating UFO sightings in Austin, Texas, when he got reports of multiple sightings in a small area of the Caribbean.

He went to Isla Tintada, the apparent center of activity. It was a typical Caribbean island, settled by wealthy people who wanted to get away from their problems in other places.

He was watching as a storm approached from seaward of his position. It was colorful and beautiful, at twilight. He took two pictures of what he assumed to be the basis of the reports. He debunked them quickly, but discovered something else in those two pictures.

And ended up dead.

"Dr. John" Matthews intended to find out how and why he died.

# Contents

# About the author

CD Moulton has traveled extensively over much of the world both in the music business, where he was a rock guitarist, songwriter and arranger and in an import/export business. He has been everything from a bar owner to auto salvage (junkyard) manager, longshoreman to high steel worker, orchid grower to landscaper, tropical fish farmer to commercial fisherman. He started writing books in 1983 and has published more than 350 books as of January 1, 2023. His most popular books to date are about research with orchids, though much of his science fiction and fantasy work has proven popular. He wrote the CD Grimes, PI series, and the Det. Nick Storie series, Clint Faraday series, and many other works.

He now resides in Gualaca, Chiriqui, Panamá, where he writes  books, plays music with friends, does research with orchids and medicinal plants. He has lately become involved in fighting for the rights of the indigenous people, who are among his closest friends, and in fighting the extreme corruption in the courts and police in Panamá.

He offers the free e-book, *Fading Paradise*, that explains what he has been through because of the corruption.


CD is the discoverer of the Chadam Protocol for curing cancer.

Facebook page Ambrosia peruviana for cancer.

Author's Note

I was in Honduras in the early sixties, where I was taking some pictures of the surrounding area at twilight. In two of the pictures there was something, I've never found just what it was, but think it was some kind of reflection in the lens. It was a Polaroid camera. It appeared to be a (sigh) saucer-shaped silver sliver between me and the mountain silhouette I was photographing. It appeared in two of the pictures, taken close together in time. There was a picture in between in which it did not appear. It was a series of four pictures of the mountain, left side and right side, then right side and left side. It appeared in the second, the right side, and fourth, the left side.

I did not see it when I took the pictures. I noticed it the following day, when I was going through the pictures taken in the past few days.

We did not have the techniques we have today that can magnify such pictures in tiny detail. I preserved those pictures for fifty five years. They were among the things stolen when some people (to use the word indiscriminately) stole land from me and destroyed much of my personal property.

I read of a supposed sighting, and remembered those old pictures. The sighting was quickly debunked, in the Caribbean case. It was not a deliberate thing. It was a kite that was caught in the winds of an approaching minor storm.

I write books. Mostly science fiction, murder mysteries, a few fact-based things, and some mild erotica.

Covers of several of my books were pictures that I didn't know I'd taken. I couldn't resist writing this one, based on something being in a picture that wasn't what the photographer meant to capture.

Or was it – but not deliberately?

Charlie Sands studied the photos of the so-called UFO sighting, and sighed deeply. Another one. Didn't these half-assed idiots who tried these silly stupidities realize that today's techniques for magnifying a digital photo, pixel by pixel, would show the nylon thread holding the thing up? Enhance the photographs at only double magnification, and you could see them. Didn't the newspaper that printed them do that simple thing?

Probably. They needed a filler, so printed it. It would be another filler when he reported what was done, and he would give them the magnified and enhanced pictures.

Charlie had started studying UFOs sightings as a teenager. He had seen some strange lights near his home when he was seventeen. He was parked by the lake with Janette, making out a bit, as they called it. Several people saw the lights, and reported them. A military-type man came to town, saying he was from Project Blue Book. He said the lights were weather balloons, and it was all a typical type of mistake people made because of the publicity of the blah, blah, blah.

Charlie saw the lights go low against a hill, then turn west and shoot up, very fast, to disappear. Weather balloons would follow an air stream, and would not make sharp turns.

He believed in flying saucers for awhile, then became more and more skeptical. He met an old woman who had taken a picture she wouldn't show to anyone. He chided her into letting him look at it, and saw it wasn't like the general type of thing that was in the papers and on TV – yet it was. It was more oval than the saucer reports. It had what could be ports. It was a dull silvery color. It was shown against a sort of reddish cliff. She said it was taken in eastern New Mexico on a vacation, four years ago. She had been smoking marijuana, and wasn't sure she wasn't somehow tricked, but she did remember the thing was sitting there, she took the picture, but it was the last frame on the roll. It suddenly shot straight up, then went into the clouds. She had gone with her companion to the spot, and there were a couple of square marks that could have been anything.

He very carefully checked the background for shadow angles and such, and the perspectives. The photo hadn't been altered, in any way he could find, and he knew how to find things, very quickly, by that time. He'd found discrepancies in dozens of such pictures. He knew where to look in modern digital photography – and it wasn't where people expected, which made finding overlays and erasures obvious. He couldn't help but notice how far down the sightings had become since digitals. Even the modern cameras were far too easy to expose any tampering or transparent lines or whatever.

There were still that very few where nothing could be found to indicate a hoax, though he knew from interviewing some of them that they were hoaxes.

That still left that same half of a percent of "unexplainable" photos. Half a percent of a thousand, and there were a lot more than a thousand, was ten. That was still a lot of smoke for there not to be a fire.

He remembered, a few years ago, when he read an editorial in a newspaper where a woman had demanded to know why, if there were intelligent beings from outer space coming here, they hadn't contacted any government, or anything.

A man had answered her with, "Because they're intelligent." She was insulted, and said that he didn't make any sense. The heated exchange went on for several issues of the new-spaper.

The final answer to her when she stated, if they're intelligent, they would contact us to make an agreement or something.

The answer: "If they're intelligent and read this paper or watch the news on television, what do they see? Rape, murder, war, larceny, malicious evil. Would an intelligent being, knowing how we are, really want to make an agreement with that kind of people? Would that being watch the crap that's in the theaters; blow up everything in sight, bombs and blood and body parts flying through the air, or sadistic murders, want to know the people that was supposedly about?

"You'll say, and it's true, that such is only the dark side of us, but that is what they'd encounter. They could travel around the world at altitude and see the wars and mayhem. They couldn't see the hundreds of people who would go to aid a child caught in an old well. It would be a short mention on TV, then the news would turn to how many were killed in the Iraqui and Afghanistan wars."

That had answered the question for him. If he went to another planet and wanted to study the beings there before attempting contact. and only saw such things, he would make his lowest priority contact.

He made the report sheet, including the pictures before and after the enhancements, and listed the discrepancies in a numbered series. He sent it to the local UFO society, who brought him there to find which of those things were hoaxes.

He called Irene, and they went to a restaurant, then to a show that was just the type of garbage he had been thinking about earlier. All the ridiculous karate crap, where any one of the blows delivered would kill a person. It was like the wrestling, where they slam and hit and kick and break chairs and furniture over each other's head, are so exhausted they can't move until "two!" when they kick out of the hold and get one as hard on the adversary – and neither has a single mark or bruise when the bout is over.

Get real!

Nobody said that anymore.

He had Irene spend the night in his hotel room. He would go back to Austin in the morning, to his regular day job. Master electrical engineer.

Maybe something would come up, somewhere. He could use a trip to Switzerland or Australia on either his hobby or his work. Maybe they would have a report from Tahiti, or somewhere.

Yeah! Right! Maybe Turtle Turd Island, if his luck got better!

He checked his computer. His e-mail.

Maybe things were going to get better! There were some sightings on a Caribbean island that he was asked to investigate!

Now, if Isla Tintada wasn't a Turtle Turd Island, maybe he would get his vacation!

Charlie stepped onto the hot tarmac from the little island hopper Cessna and looked around.

Not bad! Not bad at *all*! Tahiti pictures could have been taken there!

He didn't like the overdone ostentatious villas or chateaus or whatever they were he'd seen on the other end of the island, though. That usually meant a bunch of snobs and know-it-all pains in the ass like a few he'd met in Houston and Los Angeles.

"You're here. They said to tell you to check into the Royal Palm. It's paid," the pilot said. "It's just six blocks from the gate, or you can get a taxi. Just go straight along the entrance road and turn left at Cory Shell Road. One block. Right on the water, and not bad, if not like the fancy places on the Gotrocks End."

Charlie grinned. "Those, huh?"

"If you only knew! Half of them are here hiding from the IRS, or what have you. Spent every dime they had to get a fancier place than Richass, next door, and are in hock for the next five hundred years. You tell me why a snobby multimillionaire takes the local water taxi instead of a flight, and I'll tell you how you could probably buy and sell the lot of them."

"If I had that much, I'd be on one of these islands, but not in those overdone ostentations."

"If you've got a dime, and don't owe it, you have more than they do. They ain't got the dime, and they owe all those millions they claim they have.

"Little bar called Millie's, just this way from the hotel. Fun place, and good people."

A woman in a fur coat (On a tropical island?), sunglasses, and a lot of flashy jewelry came from the little terminal.

"Mrs 'Oh, my husband bought me *two* of those!' is to go to their little place on Jamaica. Boyfriend there. Big black with a twelve inch dong. Maybe twenty five. Hubby stays here. He's about eighty five. She's forty eight.

"Got to run!"

Charlie gave him a high five, and started toward the hotel. The natives seemed to be blacks and Latinos, and seemed friendly and open. They would stop to chat about where he was from. He had a couple of obvious pro-positions from very sexy girls, but that was part of the culture on these islands. He said he just got there, and would probably like some company after he rested a few hours. He was suffering from jet lag.

He wasn't, but he had never been the type to go for prostitutes, though he didn't hold it against them. They were just working an occupation most of them liked. As he'd had explained by a friend who was in the business, the only drawback is that she would like it all the time if it weren't for the fact that half the sick-o guys who bought her services were real cruds, and some were just plain weird and creepy.

He got to the hotel, where he looked over the clean sandstone and coquina stone place. It was nice, if a bit touristy. Inside was better and more homey to him. The fat and happy big black woman at the desk seemed to enjoy life and her job. She had a thousand jokes, if he knew the type. They would be pals. Her name was Tina.

"I'm here to investigate the flying saucer thing," he answered, when she asked him what was his occupation, or was he here for a vacation. "It's also the first vacation I've had in six years!"

"Honey, that silly-ass flying saucer thing is just that. A silly flying saucer thing. Some of those people claim to see them all the time. Some bigshit govmint man from the estados came and said they were seeing big white birds in the sun, and their minds were making them into flying saucers. Probably right.”

“Well, I’ll investigate for a week or two, then say something like that, most probably. Almost all of them are.”

“Only real flying saucer ever seen around here was when Lily was throwing the dishes at Hank when she found out he was seeing Flo on the side!”

They laughed and joked a few minutes, then she showed him his room. It was very clean and comfortable, and had a small balcony facing the gleaming blue Caribbean.

“It faces north, so you’ll like it. The ones south and east and west have the sun on them part of the day. Sun ain’t never far enough north to hit here, ‘cept the top one, and we have a little roof thing for that. Maybe ten days a year. July.

“You wants to bring a girl, it’s okay, but not loud, and not a thief. Pick ‘em up at Millie’s, and she’ll tell you which ones are no go.”

He soon took a cool shower and laid on the bed to re-read what he had. Several people had seen what they described as a large silvery metal object in the sky. No radar contacts, except twice an iffy possibility. There were no aircraft in the area, at the times. The report by the agency stated they felt people were psychologically led to think the large white birds seen in the sunlight were the bases of the reports.

He read the report of the man who came to investigate. He said he had heard the stories, and wasn't convinced, at all. He saw a flight of the white pelicans against a bright sun that looked like big white objects. He said it was explained, and went back to the states.

White pelicans were in flocks. None of the reports had mentioned more than one light. Someone who came to debunk, so did. He wasn't interested in investigating anything. His report was the first to be discounted!

About five o'clock, Charlie went down to the lobby, where he met Dr. John, who was a medical doctor by the name of John Matthews. Everyone called him Dr. John. He was a popular local character who was well-liked. He said a good restaurant was the Conch Palace. They had really good fresh seafood.

He called the number of the person he was there to meet from the local society, Jennie Prado. She would meet him at the Conch. It really did have great seafoods.

He talked with a couple of people on his way. Jennie was there, at a table by a tropical fish pool. Paul Smith, a man she knew slightly, was with her. He was interested in UFOs, in a sort of lukewarm way. He was a little condescending, but was probably alright. Jennie was about thirty, and was a little flighty, but good company. She had a great sense of humor.

They had a large meal that really was good. A sort of paella, with a slightly picante sauce. They talked about a number of things and places to go on the island. The Gotrocks End was mostly a bunch of snobby prudes, to hear them tell it, but the local pros, both male and female, could tell just how prudish they really were. They were a bunch of phony asses.

When they were getting ready to leave, Jennie handed him USB a memory stick. She had condensed all the reports for him to read. He could do a comparative cross-index search for whatever. It was a single file, with hyperlinks to individual cases.

He went to the hotel to study the reports. Jennie was thorough, and made little notes about how this or that didn't fit, or fit perfectly. It looked like she was trying to do an honest investigation. She didn't have enough to reach solid conclusions, either way. She had a list of numbers that were of reports that were debunked. It expressly didn't contain anything by or from "the US investigator (who was a pile of horse manure who couldn't investigate the pimple on his own ass)."

He spent the following day checking out the areas in the reports. Nothing definitive.

He talked with Jack Nesmith, who had filed one report. He and his wife and another couple had all signed the report. They were on the beach at about seven. The sun was just setting, and there were clouds. They watched a "football shape" in silvery gray move across a darker cloud bank for three or four minutes. It was out far enough that they couldn't make out any details, but it most certainly wasn't white birds. The clouds behind were whiter, and they were slightly gray and pink. Nesmith felt it was possibly some kind of experimental thing from the NASA relay station on Birdbeak Island, sixty miles to the north.

Just before sundown, Charlie returned to the hotel. He was in his room, and heard some excited voices outside, so stepped out on his balcony. There were three people on the next balcony who were watching something in the sky. There was a little storm coming in from the northeast, and he could see a very white spot against the clouds. It seemed to have a blue light on it.

He dodged inside and grabbed his camera. He could just make out the white object against the clouds, and snapped four pictures as fast as the digital camera would take them. It was very high resolution, so the pictures were three seconds apart. He didn't use the zoom, because that lost pixels that could be brought out, if necessary.

He would have said it was a very large white bird – except for that blue light!

It was gone. He used the maximum zoom to search, but there was nothing there but clouds.

He went back inside to make out a very concise report. He was going to take those photos apart, pixel by pixel, in the morning. This was the first time he had directly photographed any such thing.

He was, personally, positive he would find a natural explanation for this UFO, but sort of hoped he wouldn't.

He downloaded the photos from the camera, and made four copies of them on four memory sticks. He wasn't about to take the chance of losing this! He took the four gig chip from the camera, and put in another. Only four photos on a four gig chip, but he wasn't going to chance anything. He couldn't remember ever being so excited.

He loaded the special photo manipulation shop, and brought out the first photo. He examined it carefully. It was only clouds. Truly beautiful, particularly when he enhanced them, but just clouds.

The second one, he saw the object quickly. He doubled the magnification and cropped out the piece with the object. He kept the magnified picture as 2Xmpic2, and magnified the object.

It was a winged ... something. It didn't have a blue light, just an electric blue panel of some sort.

He doubled magnification again. Just the hint of pixelation, so this would be as far as he could go, with this one.

It was a somewhat crumpled ... kite? A child's kite?

Shit! He deflated. His being the first to take a provable picture of a UFO was a kite!

He brought up the next. Nothing.

Where was the kite in the first and this one?

Okay. He closed his eyes, and remembered the sequence. He started left, and moved right, for the second. Then left. Then right.

The kite would be in the fourth picture, which it was. He did the careful recording he had done with the second, and sat back. He started making out the report. It would debunk the people's sighting on the next balcony and any others that came in.

There was a slight nagging at his mind. He didn't know what it was. He had intuitions, at times, and this might be one. It would come out in its own time, but he knew damned well he was missing something.

It was one o'clock! Time for breakfast – if it wasn't already time for lunch, which it was.

Charlie chatted with a few people. He called Jennie, who said five or six people had seen the kite. It had already been reported as a kite that the wind from the approaching storm had pulled out of a boy's hands. A club spotter, John Tucker, had looked at it through his binoculars and reported it, immediately.

He looked up to see a dark cloud just to the north. There were several birds flying between, and he saw one white one that stood out, looking more like a white balloon when it turned to where the sunlight was directly on the spread wings. If he wasn't wearing polarized sunglasses, it would have looked like a big white balloon. It would *not* look like a saucer.

Not to mention, no one ever said it was white except that idiot "investigator." They said it was silvery gray.

*Nag*!

Paul Smith came into the little stand where Charlie was drinking a peach nectar drink. He said that Charlie probably had a few dozen reports of flying saucers this morning.

"The kite? I saw what that was in two minutes. Besides, it was white. White and blue."

"White?"

"All reports are of a silvery gray object. None are of a white object, except that idiot so-called investigator from the states, who reported that it was white pelicans.

"White pelicans are a flocking bird. None of the reports were about more than one object. Make up your mind what you're going to find, then say that, and go home. It doesn't have to make sense."

"Much too damned true!

"How did you learn it was a kite? Tucker?"

"No. I took pictures of it and blew them up. It was a kite. Next case?"

"Ah, yes! That would do it! Fortunate to have been using your camera, right then!"

"I wasn't. It was just inside the balcony door, so I grabbed it. Those darker clouds behind made it show up very well."

"Oh, yes. Take the picture, then use the zoom on the image. Two seconds later, you have the magnification! Don't need a photo shop for that!"

Something wasn't right about this conversation. Charlie got leery of Paul Smith. "Just before I was born, they were building a super computer. All six L six tubes. Three stories, and a whole city block. It could do ten thousand calculations per minute!

"Of course, every time they turned it on, the whole city had a brown-out. If the temperature changed, it would go nuts.

"Now, this Blackberry has a six gig memory chip, can handle sixty two million calculations per second, can contact the internet through a satellite, so you can talk to anyone in the world, anywhere in the world, works at fifty below and almost to boiling temperature, and uses a little battery whose usage couldn't be detected without special equipment.

"I don't know if it's good or bad. Regardless, it's amazing!"

"You have that one right!

"Well, happy UFO hunting! Got to run!"

*"You got that right!" is the expression. Who are you, and what are you after?*

"Catch you on the flip-flop!" Use an outdated expression, and see if he tumbles.

He got a strange look, and a raised eyebrow, then Smith was going out the door.

*So! Why are you here? What is the government doing here?*

He said that flip-flop thing off the top of his head. He got the odd look. Smith had used an identification code, he had answered it, if not perfectly, within bounds. Smith was intelligence, or CIA, or something.

Was he here because of UFOs, or because they were doing something that would look like UFOs, if you didn't know better?

Now he really did want to take another, much closer, look at those photos and their white kite!

He headed back to the hotel and to his room.

He had, long ago, learned to set little traps when he left a room, such as leaving his computer case with the zipper an inch from the end, and the pull tab laying to the left. It was laying to the right, and the zipper was a good half inch more open. The piece of toothpick on his manila files was on the floor.

And his computer was slightly warm.

Someone had searched the room and had looked at what was on his computer. His camera was still on the table by the balcony door. It was the slightest bit moved away from the lamp.

He turned it on, and hit the replay. It was erased.

He thought, then took the memory chip from the computer case carry pocket. He turned on the computer, and inserted it. He brought up the picture of the kite. It looked the same, but ... *nag*!

He read the legend. It was in lower case?

The picture number was in upper case, from the camera. It was in lower case if the picture was in any way modified.

He very carefully studied the picture. It looked the same.

He zoomed it. There was a slight distortion to the center right.

He zoomed to pixelation. That little spot was smeared.

He went to the little case to take out a second memory stick and insert it. He checked the spot that had been smeared on the first. There was a football shaped silvery object there.

His hands were shaking as he brought up the fourth picture to check for a smeared area. It was there on the one from the carry case. It showed a football shaped silvery gray object in the backup.

A small storm was approaching. Most of the sightings had been when there were lots of clouds.

To fool radar? Is that why there were those two "possibilities?" Wouldn't the higher density of the object ... but there was the stealth bomber. The object wouldn't appear on radar. It had to be seen, directly – but could be photographed!

He was the first to photograph a UFO that couldn't easily be explained away, he felt, then remembered that photo from the old woman.

He was the second – that he knew of.

Was that thing something from another world, or was it something from here? If it was from here, where did the technology come from?

This was getting a bit scary! Did Smith know?

He took out his Blackberry, and started to make a call, then thought a moment. There was pretty surely some kind of surveillance equipment in that room.

Did they now know he had a second backup? Did they know he found what they were trying to erase?

He said, "Eleven twenty three," just at bare audibility, and put the Blackberry back in his pocket. He didn't want to look too casual as he went to put the second backup chip back into the carry case. He slipped the other two out at the same time, then rummaged around to slip two unused memory chips in the case pocket. They might have counted them.

He sat at the computer to make a note that someone had erased something on the memory stick and the camera, but he had a backup, as always, so would find what it was. He had a suspicion, but couldn't see much difference in the photos. He would have to study them later.

He took a sheet of paper from his case, and went out and down to the hotel restaurant for a light lunch. He wrote a note on the paper, and took it to the desk. He got an envelope from Tina and slipped the paper and a memory chip into the envelope and addressed it to Jennie Prado. He told Tina there was a dangerous situation here, that, should anything bad happen to him, see that Jennie got that envelope. Be very careful that no one knew she had it. Do not put it with the other letters.

Tina said she had already been asked if he had left anything there for him. He was a Mr. Smith everyone knew wasn't a Mr. Smith. He might have someone watching her, so she would put a substitute envelope in the cabinet for someone else to see what happened. Maybe something for Dr. John, seeing everyone knew him.

He grinned, and said to give him a piece of notepaper. He wrote, *Hello, "Smith!" You were easy to spot. Do you work for them or us, or are you playing both ends?*

She slipped it into an envelope she wrote, *DR* on, and left it in the message cabinet. They chatted a minute, then he went back to his room. Now to see what developed.

Nothing at all, at six thirty, so he went to dinner. He was sitting in the restaurant when Smith came to sit across from him. He sat there and stared. Charlie said to drop it. What did he want.

"I have to know who 'Us' are. I can't answer if I don't. Does Dr. John know what that note's about?"

"I don't really know who 'Us' are, anymore. No."

"What did you find? Is there anything in those pictures?"

"You would know. You erased the camera and tampered with the memory chip, so you know what's supposed to be there. If it was something about that kite, I can't find it."

"Okay. I erased the camera. What about a chip? Tampered?"

"Any idiot can see when something's been done to a photo! It's lower case when it's modified, in any way!"

"Lower case?"

"The file name is listed in upper case, from the camera. When any modification is made, it's lower case."

"You modified the thing, yourself! When you cropped ... oh, shit!"

"I didn't modify the photo. I saved the cropped part as a new file, and left the photo unmodified. That means you did modify the photo, so I'll have to see if I can find out where and why. It certainly isn't something even an expert, which I am, can spot easily. It's as certainly something I can find if I have to go over those pictures pixel by pixel.

"I knew damned well you did something, and that you read all the files. I had hoped you'd left me a clue. Maybe you did, and maybe it'll be hell finding, but I will.

"Maybe I'd just drop it if it's not something sinister, or against decency, but that's not often the case when the military is involved."

"So you know you can trust me if I say it's not anything that's against, as you said, decency? If it's not some sinister plot?"

"No. You can't believe anything from another agency, and less than half from the same one."

"It's strictly defensive. I swear."

"Bullshit! It's not even the kind of thing that can be disguised as defensive!"

"It's not about military! It's about being able to move, and I don't mean down the block. I mean to the moon, or Mars, or Ganymede. They've learned how to move a lot faster than the public knows, now.

"I don't claim to know anything about it. I just know it's a matter of finding fuel. We can get there a lot faster because of inertial effects, but we can't begin to reach the velocities we need.

"The only reason the military is involved at all is funding. We have to have a dual use item. Defensive is secondary to the military mind. Offensive is priority one through ten.

"We tell them this thing can now move troops from the US to Asia in less than an hour. We intend to make it in only five minutes. We can probably do that, by now. It's easy to find fuel for anywhere here, or even to the moon. We say they can have a base on the moon that anything they fire from here or from orbit will take hours to get there, but we can get there in half an hour.

"We say we can reach nearly twenty percent of lightspeed, now, if we can solve the fuel problem. We can carry enough to reach ten percent, which ain't to sneeze at. What we learn reaching twenty percent will tell us how to reach thirty, which will tell us how to reach forty. We think we can reach about fifty four percent light-speed by the time this is done. We can go to Ganymede in a day, accounting for acceleration and deceleration."

"Fusion of free hydrogen?"

"Some kind of fusion reaction. I only know what I've taught myself. It uses something like a laser to fuse the hydrogen. After a certain speed, velocity, you start to get to the point that, no matter how much fuel you can find, you need more to move faster. Einsteinian limits."

"Which you encounter more and more of as you accelerate, so finding fuel for that is bullshit. You have half the process in that. You need the time modification part to get past a very simple fact."

"Which is?"

"You're always at rest, relative to yourself. It takes the same amount of energy to move a mile per hour faster at half lightspeed as it does at normal at-rest speed. Hell, the galaxy is already moving at a rate of fifty four thousand KPS, minimum. We're moving a thousand miles per hour on the surface of the earth from rotational velocity, the Earth is moving around the sun at umpteen thousand miles per hour.

"Each modification of velocity results in a modification of time. Time dilatation is an effect of that. It's only perception. If you believe what you've just told me, it's because they're lying in their teeth to you.

"Whatever, the only reason I can put stock into the flying saucer form is that it's the only form that will give you both effects. You have to modify your relative speed, then modify the time to where you're moving at half lightspeed, here, so to speak, and half again inside the ship. You can exceed lightspeed, relative to anything you like. You can't move, relative to yourself.

"Whatever, what's the point of the secrecy if it's not for military reasons? All your arguments fail at that question."

"You seem to know a lot about it!"

"I've been investigating this stuff for more than thirty years. I've heard all the theories, and have seen things to show what's true and what's not.

"I guess I'll have to spend some time on those photos, now. You aren't going to tell me anything. I doubt you know anything they don't want you to know."

"Be careful. You seem like an alright kind of guy. Learning too much can be dangerous."

"Yes, but to whom?"

"Probably both sides. That's what makes it so damned scary."

"Just one question. I might not have to bother with the pictures if the answer's what I'm almost sure it will be. I'll know."

"What?"

"Is it a saucer or a football?"

"That's important?"
"Yes."
"Football."
"Then they're almost as far as they're going."

Charlie went to his room to make up a PDF report with pictures and explanations, printed out a copy in full color, put it on several memory sticks, and put the whole thing in a big manila envelope. He addressed it to Jennie, then thought about it. It wouldn't mean anything to her, and she'd give it to the police if anything happened to him. The police might or might not be a good choice.

He didn't know who to give it to here. Damn!

He took the envelope, and went out. He wasn't going to leave this with Tina. He didn't want to put her in any danger.

Who had he met here he felt he could trust? He had made a big mistake in giving his hand away so fast. He should know better, by now.

He had met one person who might be one he could trust. Everyone seemed to like Dr. John, and he wouldn't have anything to gain or lose. Tina told him how to get to his office, and he went. The doctor wasn't doing anything, at the moment, so they went to the docks, to a little restaurant there, where everyone knew Dr John, and would respect his privacy. He explained what he'd learned, and what he thought. Dr. John nodded, and said he'd had a lot of suspicions about some things. It would fit, even though it did sound like a scifi movie script.

"I've made a big mistake, I think. I should have told Smith a tenth of what I did. He would figure I thought it was some of that top secret military shit that would never be practical. I could have left that idea, fairly easily. Instead, I went on and on about what a truly brilliant scientist I am that I can figure these things, and even tell them where they were off the track. Now they have to worry that I really can thwart them – or maybe someone I work for can. Someone who's way ahead of them, already!"

"Do you?"

"Not really. There's a loose organization of people who investigate this stuff who see things and theories, and can put things together. We couldn't actually make anything, but we could probably give them a basis to make something. I know enough to know that football shape won't cut it, past an early stage, and that lightspeed effects are a simple matter of position. It's mostly relative to which perception you're viewing."

"You lost me!"

"It goes back to the simple fact that you can't move relative to yourself. Relative to yourself, you're always at point neutral. You're at rest."

"I get no feeling about that. It's semantic."

"No. It's the real part. We live, consciously, in the dual relative phase. We perceive in the you-and-me position, not in the me perception. That serves us well. That bullet heading for straight between your eyes is only a perception, but we view it as a dual perception. It is only a perception, but so am I. The bullet can disarrange the me perception. Never forget that!"

"Okay. It's beyond me, now, all the way. Truth is as relative as anything else.

"What do you want from me?"

He handed him the envelope. "If anything happens to me, you can do what you think is best with this. Please don't open it unless something does happen to me. That would be, I'm afraid, a mistake as big as the one I've already made."

"Anything would have to come from Smith. You can manage to avoid any situation where he could do anything."

"I'm not worried about Smith. I'm worried about who and what he's already told. He's a flunky who's been handed a line."

"I see. They have to worry about who and what you've told."

"Yes, but not here."

"I agree that I'm not in any danger from whoever for whatever reason.

"What now?"

"I have to get the information in that envelope to some people."

"Who?"

"I don't have any idea."

Charlie soon went back to the hotel. He hoped he'd be left alone, but didn't really think he would. He felt he had about forty eight hours to survive, then they'd leave him alone. That would be time enough that they would know damned well any information he had was out.

He went out for dinner, then around town in places there were a lot of people. He felt he would be safe enough in a crowd.

He went back to the hotel, and to his room. There was no evidence that he was searched again. He'd made it plain enough it would be pointless.

He showered and laid out some clothes for the morning, then went out on his balcony to look at the stars and wonder if there really was someone from a planet with an orbit around one of them

who was here, studying him and his society –
and wondering how it had gone so wrong.

He sighed, and turned to go back inside.

"It was just after midnight when he came back, then Liam found him here when he came to work this morning. He fell behind the hedge, so no one saw him until they ... well," Tina said to Captain Harding, of the police. "If he fell a little farther out, the hedge might have saved him. He hit right on the concrete. Four floors."

Harding looked up to the balconies. It seemed cut and dried. He came in a little after midnight, so was probably pretty drunk. He went out on the balcony. Probably sat on the wide railing, fell. Goodbye, Charlie! The same thing happened to that woman, three months ago, but on the other side of the hotel. Get drunk and sit on a railing three or four floors above a concrete slab!

Dr. John came in, and asked what was up? He was the closest thing they had to a medical examiner, though this one was as obvious as the last.

Harding pointed to the body. Dr. John went over, and groaned. He said he knew the guy.

"Well, drank a bit much, fell off the railing," Harding said. "Look like that to you?"

"It's supposed to, but he didn't drink. He had a peach nectar while I had a beer. He said he just didn't like the effects."

"Well, that's your job. I have to file that it looks like an accidental death."

Dr. John went to the body to examine the damage. His left shoulder took the brunt of the fall. It was broken, and the bone was protruding a bit.

Then why was the right side of the head caved in?

He looked up at the balcony, and said not to touch or move anything until he was back. He went up to Charlie's room, where he noted there was no computer or case or camera that Charlie had told him about. He stepped out onto the balcony, and saw where something was wiped up from the floor, and from a spot on the rail. He took sample swabs, but knew it was blood that was washed away, there.

He went back down, and said it was murder, that there was plenty of evidence of that on the balcony, that some items he knew were there yesterday afternoon were missing

Harding didn't seem to appreciate the statement, but his job was to investigate it as murder after the ME proclaimed it to be such. He took a crew to the room. Matthews finished with what he could find, and told the ambulance crew to take the body to the clinic for the autopsy.

Then Dr. John went to his office and to the file cabinet he kept the office expenses and such in to retrieve the manila envelope Charlie had given him.

*I don't know what they plan. I think they will try to get me away from here and to say the sightings here were kites and pelicans. I will not say that when I know it is not true.*

*A man called Paul Smith here is an agent, but for which agency I have not been able to determine. It is fifty percent in my mind that his own agency is misleading him. He is filled with science facts and theories that are incomplete. If their research is limited to what they have done and what they told him it will be a very limited success.*

*I find I can't quite trust others who caused my coming here. There is that piece here and there that doesn't seem to fit with other things. Why is someone who you can only describe as "flighty" in charge of this kind of organization? Why was another so anxious for me to know an object seen was merely a kite when it would so soon become obvious? Why try to delay me from investigating?*

*Their basic aim is to be able to reach a good percent of lightspeed. What they have and the theories under which it works will suffice for movement within the solar system. It will suffice to be able to reach Mars in six hours instead of six minutes. The mini-fusion propellant. The basic design may well operate to specifications.*

*Their recipe lacks a critical ingredient that I will not discuss here. I am merely laying a background explanation.*

*I have, if unwittingly, made myself a fly in their ointment. They will not take the time to consider the reactions to their actions. They will believe they can get me out of the way quickly enough to where what is in this envelope is not released.*

*Make no mistake! They will act as the military mind always acts! They will probably kill me and will also kill you if you aren't able to disburse the information included herein widely. It is a case in which speed, albeit of another description, is vital.*

*I have learned everything included here through personal study. Everything is somewhere on the internet. Anyone on this planet may do the same, and many undoubtably have. The military mind will seek secrecy and that kind of silliness in lieu of thought and logic.*

*Anyone can design what they are producing. It is a matter of funding, at this stage. If a small bit of cooperation could replace the personal greeds of the people involved this would have been done, I estimate, circa 1998-2000. A bit of interagency cooperation instead of competition would have the complete answer instead of two agencies, each with a third. The final third is synergic.*

*Be that as it may, what you must have notice of made widely available is in the two photographs included. The memory stick has copies of the original photos you can copy to use various enhancement programs with, though such is not necessary. The simplest photo shop will decrease mid tones to where the object stands out quite clearly and the great pixel content assures that magnification of sixteen to seventeen times will show very clearly what is there.*

*Take photo 1 and note that it is a photo of a white kite with a blue panel on it. That kite was the focus, but the distance made focus a bit less critical.*

*Consider that the kite is at the centerpoint of a clock face. Look at 10:00 halfway to the edge and you will see a slightly more silvery gray spot, football shaped.*

*Photo 2; look at a little past 1:00 halfway to the edge and you will see the same object.*

*Magnify and enhance slightly and you will see what this obviously is. It is a picture of a UFO, taken accidentally – in both cases.*

*I do not know how the object remains in air. That it is not a dirigible is made more than plain by the fact the object is in the clouds in a storm where the winds at that altitude would exceed a hundred miles per hour, easily.*

*I estimate the photos were taken six seconds apart. Note the distance the object moved in that time. The kite was between and the winds in that area were probably in excess of 60MPH. The object is perhaps a mile and a half farther away. The kite was perhaps a mile and a half away. The object moved, I estimate, four and a half miles in six seconds. 1.5 MPS. 90MPM. 5,400MPH.*

*The object would not be visible to the naked eye except in very rare flashes when it was passing a darker cloud. It is so nearly the color of the clouds that it becomes even harder to distinguish, plus it is moving at a speed the eye can only rarely follow. Were it white or a bright color that contrasts with the clouds it would appear a streak of color, much like a meteorite.*

*I believe the craft is unmanned. No animal body could hope to withstand the immense gravitational-like stresses of acceleration.*

*There are reports starting in the 1950's that such objects made right angle turns. That would be handled by the second part of the design, which, so far, this one ignores.*

*My quest here is not to stop the research. We can have the stars, but not so long as it is a series of top secret military madness schemes.*

*See the enclosed memory stick.*

*Charles Downing Sands*

Dr. John put the items back into the envelope, after examining the photographs. He could just make out the object, and didn't doubt it would be exactly as described, when enhanced.

He was going to try to get the information spread. That could best be done through the internet. Hit about twenty science forums and information sites at once. If one managed to keep it, this might work.

Okay. Charlie didn't think Smith was behind his death. Dr. John wasn't nearly so sure.

If some military organization was behind it, it was going to be both dangerous and difficult. Harding was already determined it would be called an accident. He didn't have the skills to investigate anything like this, and would want it to go away.

Dr. John Harold Matthews wasn't so easy to manipulate. He wasn't in the least afraid of the military, USA or other. He knew enough of the psychology behind the thought patterns that he could use to hold them at bay.

He hoped.

Whatever, he would give them a run for their money!

He thought a little longer and deeper. He was first considering having the people on the UFO club get the information out, but Charlie didn't trust them. It was pretty obvious that Jennie, as much as he tended to like her, seemed flighty. At times. He had also seen her very much the organized woman.

Who had hurried to Charlie with the information that the object sighted was a kite? Had he known Charlie had taken photographs, and didn't want those photographs lookcd at too closely? Could he know that one or two pictures of a kite may have an object moving five thousand miles per hour in one of them, much less two?

How did that camera capture an object moving at that speed, at all?

He could grant that. Charlie was an investigator, and had paid a lot of money for a special camera. That some newer digitals had that much shutter speed was known. They captured the exact screen as the button was pushed. A thousandth of a second, or less, if the literature could be believed. He'd seen pictures of a high muzzle-velocity bullet leaving the pistol, about a quarter inch from the barrel, and you could make out the very clear rifling pattern, and the smoke was like a painting. Not even a little blurry.

He took out the photos again, and looked. There was the slightest blurring of the object. Everything else was sharp and clear.

Five thousand miles per hour. A thousandth of a second shutter speed. The object had moved about fourteen inches, in that time. The tiny blurring would fit perfectly.

They had to get their hands on all the copies of those photos. The originals would show an expert that they weren't produced in some lab. They were not overlain. They were not tampered with, in any way. They were exactly as taken.

Well, Harding was going to give up before he started on this. Dr. John would never let it go. He was going to find who killed Charlie Sands.

  He wished he had some experience in this kind
of thing. He did know how to get the information out.

Dr. John called on Harding to see what his crew had found. As he suspected would be the case, nothing. No, there was nothing to be found in the room. No, they hadn't taken fingerprints there. It was a hotel room. There were hundreds of prints, probably. No, they hadn't taken pictures. No, they hadn't taken samples from the moisture on the balcony. It rained a little during the night. It was probably just rainwater.

"Look, Doc. We always got along well. Don't get all het up about some guy getting drunk and falling off a balcony. We have enough to do without having to investigate that kind of thing."

"He wasn't drunk. His blood alcohol was zero. He didn't get his head caved in from the fall. He hit on the other side, on the shoulder. Those balconies are stacked, and there was no rainwater on any except the top one, and that on the other side of the building.

"The cranial damage was from a rounded heavy item, probably a piece of two and a half inch pipe."

"So he fell and his head hit the rail on the next lower balcony. You're trying to manufacture a case."

"No. I'm doing what I swore to do when I took the job as medical examiner. I'm looking at the evidence, objectively, and trying to find the most logical explanation. I'm not refusing to investigate, and I'm not manufacturing rails on balconies that don't have the type, or raining in a couple of spots on a balcony that wouldn't get any rain on it."

"Christ! So somebody spilled a glass of water on a balcony! That doesn't mean murder!"

"Definitely not, if you can produce the glass or container."

"He took it back inside."

"Then went out to climb on a rail and fall off when he was cold sober and didn't have a trace of any drug in the cadaver."

Harding shrugged.

"Okay. I'll file my report, including what I found at the scene, and the fact you've refused to investigate. I'll let the council figure out why you won't investigate, for themselves. See if they come to the same conclusion."

He left before he got really pissed. Had Harding sold out?

It sure as hell looked like it!

He was going to rue the day he did. He wasn't the world's best cop, to start with. This showed that he was either totally incompetent or totally crooked.

Or intimidated?

How do you investigate this kind of thing? Where do you go, after finding evidence that a hundred percent points to murder?

Be logical: Someone was in that room.

That someone carried a piece of pipe, or a truncheon of some sort, into that room – or was it still there?

It would be somewhere in the hotel.

That someone took a computer and case and a camera and case out of that room.

It had to do with the UFO. That limited who it could be.

This was going nowhere.

He went to his file cabinet, and looked at the contract to be medical examiner. It made him an official police officer with special powers. In cases of violent death, he could declare himself in charge, in cases where his expertise was more to blah, blah, blah.

He headed for the hotel. Tina said the room hadn't been entered since Harding left, after being in it for three minutes. He said he had to look around that room, and in certain places in the hotel. That Charlie had been murdered, and that Harding was refusing to investigate.

"I didn't think he was the kind to get drunk, much less so bad he fell off a balcony he would have to climb up on the rail. He liked to joke, and was nice."

"Did anyone come to see him here?"

"Well, that Smith person, and John Tucker came, once, when he wasn't here. They didn't come any other time when I was out front or I would have seen them. Some people from that UFO thing came, but I don't think they were here to see him."

He went into the room and looked around. He suspected it had already been searched a lot more thoroughly than he knew how to do it. Maybe more than once.

He went out on the balcony, and looked around and down. He had to lean out to see the spot Charlie's body had hit. There were some trash containers by the door to the utility room at the end of the building, and the concrete slab, and the hedge.

Something occurred to him. He took out his cell phone and looked up Charlie's number. He called it. It rang, but there was no answer. He could just barely hear a cellular ringing in the distance below.

Charlie's phone wasn't in the room, and wasn't on the body.

He raced downstairs and out to the side under the balcony, then on to the end by the trash barrels. He called Charlie's number again. The phone rang, the sound coming from the trash barrels.

He put on the latex gloves he always carried and went through the barrel the sound came from. The phone was just under a layer of scrap papers that had been dumped in during the past few minutes. He took it out, and went to the other barrel, but there was nothing in it. He expected there would be a piece of pipe.

He put the cellular in a plastic bag, and looked around.

The utility room door. Someone came through that door, and was going out to the body when something happened that made them dump the phone.

Someone came out? He opened the door, and looked in.

The utility room! That would be the place to stow the pipe!

He stopped to think.

The door slammed shut. It was a light door, and he had left it open when he came in. A little breeze, and it slammed shut.

He tried to open it. It was locked.

Okay! He opened it easily, first time. It slammed shut, and was now locked.

He went around, and came in through the hotel. Pete Parker, the handyman for the hotel, was in the hall. He stopped to ask about the door.

"Yeah. Got to remember it locks if you push it all the way. Two phase lock. One click, and it'll open again. Two, and it'll lock.

"When you go out and you might come back, you close it easy. One click. If you ain't coming back, or it's night, you close it hard. Two clicks. It locks automatic, like."

He went into the room, and looked around. There wasn't anything obvious. There were some sections of pipe on a shelf in a cubby. A couple of inches to a meter.

He checked. There was an eighteen inch nipple of two and a half. It was among several odd sizes.

It was damp. The rest were very dry.

He took it, and slipped it into an evidence bag. It was iron. There was no way to get all the blood out of iron. This was the murder weapon, and he could probably prove it.

He stood, thinking.

Charlie was killed and pushed over the rail. If he was close to the rail, a small person or woman could do it. Hit him and push. Maybe lift a little. If he was on the rail, lift a leg, and he would go over.

Clean up what you could of the blood on the balcony.

Grab the comp and camera and whatever.

After midnight. No one is in the halls. Slip out, and go down the service stairs that go out by the utility room door.

Slip the pipe into the cubbyhole.

What next? Why go ... you hear a phone. You don't want the body discovered until you've had time to get away, unnoticed.

You run out the utility room door, leaving it open so you can run back in.

You get the phone, and head back to the utility room. There is a little drizzle of rain, and a breeze with it. The door slams shut. You can't get back inside.

You ditch the phone, and go around front, to come in again. The computer and camera are in the utility room.

Wait a minute! You came before midnight to get inside the hotel while the door was open. After midnight, the door is closed, and you have to be buzzed in! You will certainly be noted and remembered!

Either the computer and camera are still in here, or you came back this morning for them. If you came back for them, you would be noticed ... or not!

"Pete! Can you hear me?"

"Yo!"

"Did you go out the utility room door this morning and leave it on half lock?"

"No!"

Okay. You come back, get the computer and camera, and close the door as you leave, very quietly. It's unlocked for me to open.

This is all stupid!

But it's also logical.

Another thing! You had to come in early this morning. Someone will have seen you!

It would have to be before Pete came to work. He would go into the utility room, and there would be an expensive computer and a more expensive camera, sitting right there. That must *not* happen!

"Pete!"

"Yo, Doc?"

"What time do you start work in the mornings? This morning?"

"Seven. Here at a quarter to."

"What time do the lobby doors open for the public?"

"Five. The Puerto Rico flight leaves at six."

"It does ... so what?"

"Got to be there half an hour. People want to catch it, they have to leave at five here. Don't want to have to buzz the people in and out."

Five to six thirty.

Now to see who came into the hotel at five to six thirty and didn't leave.

"Oh, yeah! Doc?" Pete called.

"Yes?"

"I did go out this morning to dump stuff in the trash."

Shit!

Well, does that really change anything?

No. Not really.

He went to the front desk. Tina said there were a lot of people this morning. Four people were leaving on the seven o'clock to Puerto Rico, and a lot of people came to say goodbye.

"Who? Were they carrying anything?"

"People from that silly UFO thing. And the WorldRiders, and some other club. Six or seven of them. They didn't carry anything in. They helped carry things out."

Okay. What was changed?

Nothing. He could believe his earlier scenario, because of that cellular.

"Was Smith among them?"

"I don't think so. I didn't see everyone, and they may have been here for something else."

"Something else?"

"Yeah. I had to go to a couple of rooms to wake them up. I saw that UFO woman and her buddy in the hall. They were leaving, and she had some things I assumed were for the people on the flight."

"A computer and a camera?"

"Computer? Well, yes. Tucker was carrying something else, I think. I didn't really pay any attention. I can't stop every ... oh!"

"Tina! Listen to me! If anyone, including the sheriff, asks what you told me, it was about going ahead and using Charlie's room! Get that straight! You do not remember if you saw anybody specific in the halls this morning. All those people were in and out, and you didn't pay any attention to any of them! Got it?"

"Doc, I have, as you say, got it!"

He went back to the utility room, picked up his evidence bags, and went back to his office. He found the blood on the pipe with the phenolpthalien test. There wasn't enough to type, but there wasn't much doubt whose blood it was. There were blood traces in the swabs he'd taken from the balcony. There were no prints on anything.

He went to the Gotrocks End, just before the steel-gated entrance road, to Jennie Prado's place. He parked his Hyundai outside, and went to the door. She opened it as he came onto the porch, and said to come on in.

Harding and Tucker were sitting there. Harding had his pistol laying in his lap.

"Don't do anything too stupid," Dr. John said. "If I don't stop it, the whole mess goes to forty one websites. Automatically."

"We can't allow that!" Jennie snapped.

"You can't stop that!" Dr. John fired back.

"Listen," Tucker said. "We can't let others get this technology first! Do you know what they could do?!"

"About what you plan doing, I would imagine. Military, excuse the oxymoron, minds think alike – or fail to think – alike, I should say."

"What did Sands really know about the project?" Tucker asked. "We had a ... device ... that enabled us to overhear a few conversations. It was chilling to hear him speak to Smith, one time. He seemed to have intimate knowledge of what we were doing."

"He used the web to research UFO sightings. That led to talking with people. That led to other types of research. That led to mini-fusion laser techniques. That led to fusion driven ram drives. That led to learning something about physics. That led to theorizing how to utilize the several technologies. That led to combining some. That led to the fact, as he described it to me, that the omniverse is a capacitor effect. That led to time and motion studies, which soon showed them to be the same thing, and the only things that the omniverse is built on. That led to a theory of how to combine three or four technologies, instead of just two. That led to his belief that UFOs were, at least, possible. That led to him coming here. That led to him being killed so his ideas won't be investigated or researched, now.

"I think he could have put you at least fifty years ahead of your competition. You killed the goose."

"He would have given them the technology?" Jennie asked.

"What the...! He didn't have any technology, or any way to use his theories! He just worked them up to see how close he could come to doing what you're doing, if he had the funding. And knowledge. He was working from general principles, not specific!"

"He was a genius," Tucker said, sadly.

"Who you killed, making you morons, or worse. Certainly immensely stupid."

"That wasn't our idea! It was under orders!" Jennie cried.

"Making you even more stupid! If you knew it was a stupid decision, but did it anyhow, you're stupid squared!"

"We don't have a choice in the matter," Tucker said. "You know they can shut down the web? Then, how will you get that information spread?"

"You *can't* be that stupid! *Nobody* could be that stupid!"

"What do you mean?"

"What would happen to transportation, banking, communications, medicine, and everything else, if the net were shut down for, say, one hour? What happens to the economy of any major country?"

"They would keep certain functions through the satellites," Jennie said.

"You *are* an airhead. The science nets would have to remain operative to keep those specific frequencies operative, so you would accomplish nothing at all, other than to destroy the entire infra-structure of your cities.

"Consider one other thing. (He was making it up as he went.) To permanently install a program in your personal computer, you shut it down, and restart it."

"I don't get...?" Jennie started.

"Yeep!" from Tucker.

"You now have to wonder if shutting down the net would permanently install the information on any of thousands of websites.

"I'll go now. Just one more question.

"Which  one of you killed Charlie?"

"I did," Jennie answered. "It was in panic. I thought he represented someone else."

"Then the bunch of you will get the hell off of Isla Tintada, and never return. The first time any of your agencies try to use the crap you intend putting into space, that information hits the web, in spades. It will contain one page that isn't in those computer records. It will basically tell them how to combine four technologies into one ship that will defeat anything you can conceive of."

"Then he did have a way," Jennie said.

"It's not even difficult. Get out!

"Oh! Harding! You have to resign for personal reasons, and will go with them."

He walked out, and got in his car. He drove to the clinic, where he finished what he was doing on the little hidden notebook computer, and sent it. He then went home to clean up and rest for a couple of hours. He was back in his office at four, when Smith and a general, in uniform, yet, marched (literally!) into the office. Smith was two feet behind the general, where the ass couldn't see the grin Smith sent to Doc.

"I'm Major General Franklin Tethers, United States Air Force!"

"Big fucking deal. I'm Dr. John.

"Hello, Smith. How's the world been treating you?"

"Can't complain."

"Coffee? General Feathers?"

"We're not here to drink your damned coffee!" Tethers snapped.

"Well, it's my break time, so you can either join me or leave."

"You'd better get this, and get it straight, and fast! I don't have time to chatter with some local practitioner!"

Dr. John stood, and faced the general. "Sit down and shut the fuck up!"

"Who do you think..?!"

"Now! The only general you are here is a general shithead!"

"Er?" he sat on the straight back chair.

"Coffee, Smith? General Weathers?"

Smith was having a hard time not laughing. Tethers looked like he was having a heart attack. Smith didn't dare try to talk. He nodded.

"Black?" he nodded again.

"Smithers?"

"Er. With cream, please."

Dr. John poured the coffee, and put cream and sugar on the desk for them. He sat.

"I hope the weather's been as good where you came from as it has been here! Smith can tell you how this place is. When the weather's bad, it's still good!"

Tethers broke out laughing until tears were rolling down his face. "You actually scare the holy living piss out of me! Big bad General Shithead, that's me! I'll intimidate you until you crawl and beg me not to do any of the horrible things I say I'll do!

"Gord, is this office bugged?"

"Of course. I can turn it off, and can have an accident with the recorder."

Tethers nodded. Smith took out his cellular to punch a number. "It's all dead, now."

"Well, Doc! May I call you Doc? Call me Frank."

Smith shook his head, just the least bit, behind Tether's back.

"Whatever. What do you want?"

"It's not what I want, it's what they, who will remain nameless, want. Just some assurances."

"I've stated it the way it is."

"Look. I believe you. I'm sure Gordy believes you. They won't."

"And?"

"They want a copy of the last sheet," Smith said. "Just say what you want to say, General."

"The last sheet was mentioned just to let you know there was more. It isn't one sheet. It's a sort of set of diagrams. Charlie says it's just a theory, but there isn't any reason it won't work. He's tried the parts he was equipped to try, and everything was exactly to the theory.

"I will *not* give you those diagrams. I'll make a printout of the last sheet for you."

Tethers started to say something. Smith said that would do, he was sure.

"I'll have to go someplace else to use some other equipment. I'm sure you understand why I won't use anything here."

"Will do," Smith said. "How long?"

"Meet me here in the morning, at eight."

They agreed, and left. Dr. John watched through the spy camera he had put in the bush out front as they went to the car at the curb, and got in. It went a few meters along the street, and Smith got out and went to the sidewalk. The general drove away. Dr. John grinned. He went out, locked the office, got in his car, and drove away, in the opposite direction from where Smith was waiting in the bushes. He watched as Smith pulled a motor scooter out of the hedge and started toward where he was just turning the corner. He went to the next block and turned onto a side street. A moment later, Smith flew by on the scooter. He waited, and went back to the main road and into town near the marina. He had a boat there he was sure was bugged in every conceivable way. He parked by the gate, and walked down the road to a little café, where he sat to order coffee and a pecan Danish.

He walked the three blocks to the hotel, and asked Tina to give him the package in the closet, and to let him use a small room somewhere no one would know he was. If anyone asked, he had come through and gone on down to the beach, so far as she knew.

He took the notebook computer and little printer into the room and made out a convincing sheet. When no one was around, he took the computer and printer back for Tina to put in the cabinet under the name Gerald Jones.

He went back to the marina, and watched as Smith would come to the gate to look at his car, then would go back to the docks. He slipped into the marina, and made his way through some sea grapes and mangroves to the tackle shed. When he saw Smith coming in off the dock, he went down and out the door, just as Smith went past. He timed it, and was just getting to the road by the gate when Smith was returning. Smith stepped into the hedge by the gate, and he went by and to his car. He spent the rest of the day calling on patients. Smith had to be bored out of his skull!

Then he went home to bed.

Smith and the general came into the office at eight sharp. Dr. John was with Mrs. Grantley, finished her health form for the insurance, and sent her on. He sat at his desk to fill out the rest of the office call form, put it in the file, and sat again. He didn't say anything until he took a legal-sized sheet from the desk drawer and handed it to Smith, who looked tired.

"I only said the last sheet. The whole instruction thing was four diagrams, and another sheet."

Tethers grunted, and looked at the sheet.

*from dgm. 2. As you will note, the connection is mostly the fact it is there. It needs no direct connection. The drive is electronic and induced through the magnetic driver.*

*Step 9: the fusion drive is placed at two spots exactly 90 degrees apart from the center of the axis. The earlier explained spin directs the power input, putting the drive effect at 45 degrees, the most efficient display as shown in the gravity box. With this simple device one may exceed lightspeed. You are not moving in either of two directions at more than two thirds lightspeed, but the tack effect moves you at 1.2 lightspeed.*

*I have not the ability to produce parts that will withstand the stresses induced, but the fact you are actually moving in two intersticed inertial fields reduces the stresses by half. One remembers that one is always at rest relative to oneself.*

*Step 10: This may prove the most difficult part or it may as well prove the most easily done.*

*You are in a position where you will wish to move other than at a straight line. You will, because of the effect of the time distortion device, be able to move at will along the major axis, though "Tilting" the ship will prove as much as impossible. You may, in short, move up or down or may move at a ninety degree angle to that axis in any direction. For this, it will be necessary to select the straight line flight that will put you where you wish to go when the place you wish to go will be there, the same as going to Mars. You don't aim for where Mars is, you aim for where it will be.*

*I am quite sure this will prove a very minor point, but remain wary of easy solutions. Missing a target one degree at twenty feet is a lot different from missing by one degree at five lightyears!*

*That's about it. You can see there has been a lot of research on several phases and almost none on combining the phases. It should prove a very workable kind of thing.*

*I believe, if the world changes radically to where people will work together for the good of the race, this can happen in ten to twelve years. At today's sick pace, it will happen in forty to fifty years. Society can cope with the truth of what we are.*

*We are time and motion. That is all.*

"But this doesn't tell us how to do it!" Tethers exclaimed.

"I specifically told you it didn't. You have to see the diagrams and the first part."

"We could get it from you," Smith warned. "I like you. Don't make us do that!"

"You could get it from me easily enough," Dr. John agreed. "The result will be that everyone gets it. Only I can stop that. I've had hypnotic sessions that guarantee that, should you try any of that crap, my memory of how to stop it will be erased. Go for it, if you think you and your little project will survive.

"The very best you would have then is being among the top five or so who have it, and the stalemate to actual progress will continue.

"There's a specific time I have to do a specific thing, and it's a thing I do regularly, anyhow. It's a matter of exactly when I do it.

"You'd be smart to get the hell out of my face."

"Doc, why won't you let your own country have this one thing? Why do you have something like this hanging over all our heads?" Smith asked.

"Because, without it, Charlie, a very good man, died for nothing. If he were still alive, he would probably give it to you in the mistaken belief you're different from the others, who are, in reality, clones of you.

"Think about it. Use your methods, and you *will* fail. Don't, and you have the same chance you did when this started."

They looked at each other. Tethers started to color, so Dr. John knew there was going to be another tirade. He would revert back to the thing he was when he first came to the office. Smith saw it, and said, sharply, "You win! Let's get out of here!"

They left. Abruptly.

Dr. John let a long breath escape, and sat back. He could hope this one worked. He soon got up and went outside and to near the street.

He took out his phone, and called a number. Jack Nesmith, who he had met a long time ago, and who was with a society dedicated to stopping the war mentality insanity that was sweeping the world, answered.

"I think I pulled it off."

"Thank God for that! How did you do it?"

"I lied."


C. D. Moulton's works are available on most major outlets as printed or e-books. CD writes the CD Grimes, PI mysteries, the Det. Lt. Nick Storie mysteries, the Clint Faraday mysteries, the Flight of the Maita science fiction series, books on orchid culture and many others of many types. Mystery, adventure, intrigue, science fiction, fantasy, paranormal, mild erotica, and factual.